D0537955

MONSTER TRUCKS

BOLT

SPEED - 100	
BRAINS - 72	
POWER - 65	
SKILL - bravery	

Bolt loves nothing more than racing and will do anything for his monster mates – except their homework!

MONSTER TRUCKS

FIZZ

SPEED - 99	
BRAINS - 65	
POWER - 30	
SKILL - fast loop-the-loops	

Step aside, here's Fizz! Small but speedy, Fizz is three-time winner of the Trucksville Drift & Style Cup.

MONSTER TRUCKS

NEWTON

SPEED - 95	
BRAINS - 100	
POWER - 42	
SKILL - speaks 60 languages	

Newton's brain is more powerful than a top-notch computer and he has a stylish crash helmet.

CHUNK

SPEED - 91
BRAINS - 22
POWER - 100
SKILL - pie-eating champion

Everyone loves Chunk! His brain is the size of a ping pong ball but he has a heart of pure gold.

ROXY

SPEED - 98
BRAINS - 89
POWER - 64
SKILL - skatepark champion

Streetwise Roxy is the queen of the skatepark and can successfully land a triple backflip.

MASHER

SPEED - 100
BRAINS - 67
POWER - 76
SKILL - cheeky pranks

Loud, fast and rather smelly, Masher is everyone's favourite bad boy. But not when he bends the rules…

For Tash, Darcy, George and the new arrival.
Can't wait to meet you little buddy.
J.H.

For all fans of trucks, fun, and rock and roll!
TADO

First published in 2015 by Scholastic Children's Books
Euston House, 24 Eversholt Street
London NW1 1DB
a division of Scholastic Ltd
www.scholastic.co.uk
London ~ New York ~ Toronto ~ Sydney ~ Auckland
Mexico City ~ New Delhi ~ Hong Kong

Text copyright © 2015 Jon Hinton
Illustrations copyright © 2015 TADO

PB ISBN 978 1407 14699 7

MONSTER TRUCKS

Mega City Cup

Written by **Jon Hinton**

Illustrated by **TADO**

SCHOLASTIC

The Monster Trucks were racing at Mega City. A huge crowd of monsters of all shapes and sizes had come along to cheer on their favourite trucks: Masher, Chunk, Newton, Roxy, Fizz and Bolt.

Bolt was having a great time whizzing along the zig-zaggy track as he overtook Fizz, Roxy and Newton.

Suddenly, SCREEETCH!
Bolt slammed on his brakes.

Chunk was at the side of the road eating **popcorn**.
"Hey buddy," called Chunk. "This popcorn is super **yummY** — do you want some?"
"No thanks," laughed Bolt as he zoomed off.
"We're meant to be racing, not snacking!"

Chunk joined the race again — although he loaded up with extra popcorn first!

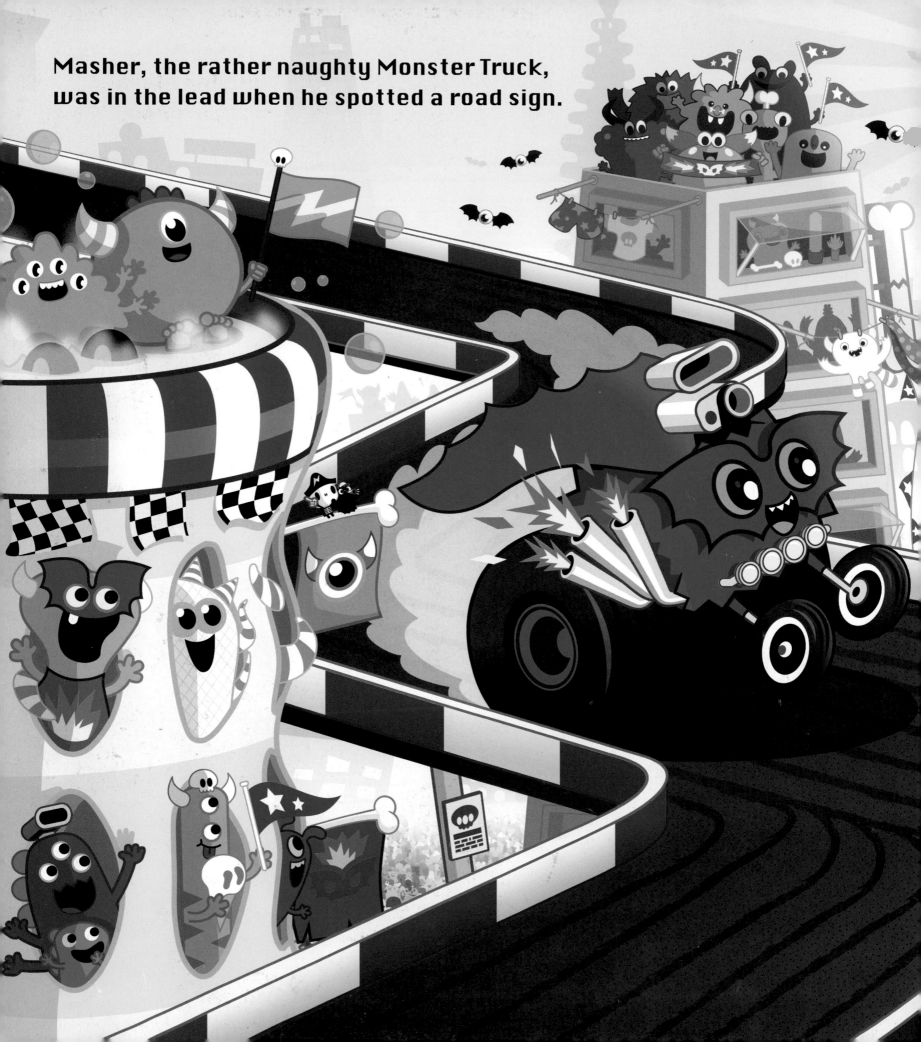

Masher, the rather naughty Monster Truck, was in the lead when he spotted a road sign.

"He he he," giggled Masher as he switched the sign around. "They'll never catch me now!"

FINISH

FINISH

ROOOOARRR! The Monster Trucks were tearing through the city as fast as their giant wheels could carry them.
"This way everyone!" yelled Bolt.
Oh no! Bolt, Fizz, Roxy and Newton followed Masher's road sign.

Chunk, however, was far too busy enjoying his popcorn and did not notice the road sign — or his four friends heading in totally the wrong direction!

Bolt, Fizz, Newton and Roxy were stuck in a **traffic jam.**
"This can't be right," huffed Fizz. "We must have taken
a wrong turn. We'll never catch Masher up now!"
"Don't worry," said Newton, studying his computer.
"I have a plan…"

Newton led his three friends onto the **skate line.**
"This should take us right back into the race,"
announced Newton as they zipped along
amongst the Skatemonsters.

"Yee-haa!"

"Yee-haa!" yelled Bolt as the four monster mates shot off the skate line and chased Masher and Chunk into a long, dark tunnel.

Back in the bright sunlight, the monsters zoomed towards
the finish line. Masher was in the lead, closely followed by Bolt,
Fizz, Roxy and Newton. ROOARRR! Bolt gave one final push,
but it was too late... Masher was going to win!

WHOOSH! Something small, purple and very very fast appeared. It was Fizz!

"Go Fizz, go!" yelled Bolt as Fizz drifted past a furious looking Masher and crossed the finish line to win the race.

Hooray!

Bolt was about to cross the finish line to claim third place
when, once again...
SCREEETCH! He slammed on his brakes.
"Bolt, why have you stopped?" asked Roxy and Newton.
"It's Chunk," gasped Bolt. "He's disappeared!"

"Chunk must be in the **tunnel**," said Newton as the three friends shot back along the racetrack in search of him.

With their headlights on, the Monster Trucks searched the dark tunnel for their giant red friend. But there was no sign of him. Where could he be? **CRUNCH!** "I just rolled over something," yelled Roxy. **"Hey...**

Following the trail of popcorn, Bolt, Roxy and Newton raced through the long, gloomy tunnel.

They powered up a steep hill...

CRUNCH...
CRUNCH...
CRUNCH...

They whizzed down a steep hill, CRUNCH...
CRUNCH...
CRUNCH...

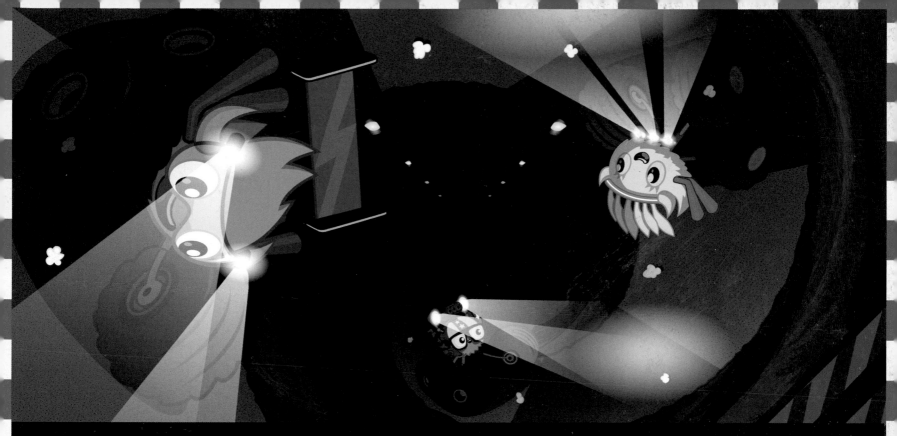

They zipped through a loop the loop. CRUNCH, CRUNCH, CRUNCH...

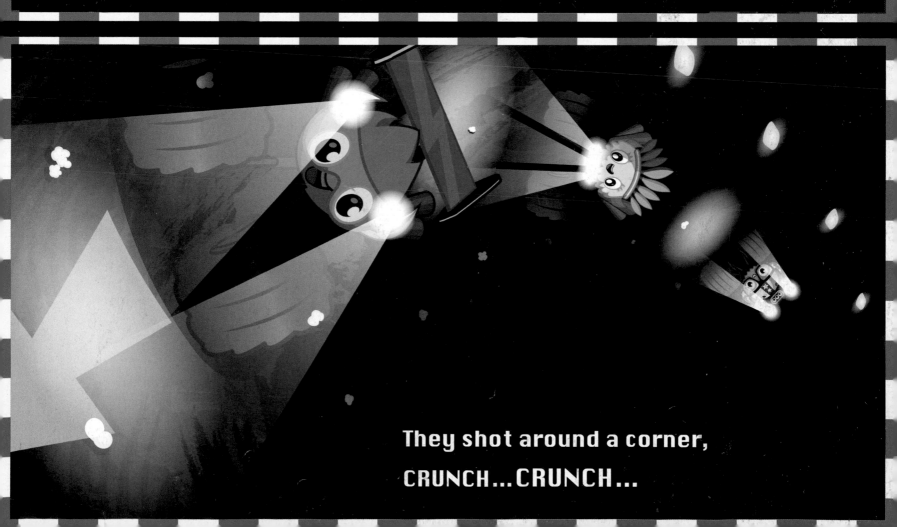

They shot around a corner,
CRUNCH...CRUNCH...

"CHUNK!" laughed everyone together.
"Thanks for coming to find me, guys. I didn't think I would **ever** find my way out of the tunnel," said a very grateful Chunk. "But I'm really sorry you didn't get to finish the race."

"Never mind," replied Bolt. "Racing is fun, but **friends** are far more important!"

"Sorry I cheated," mumbled Masher, but no one heard as they were too busy shouting, "Well done Fizz!"

MONSTER TRUCKS

BOLT
SPEED - 100
BRAINS - 72
POWER - 65
SKILL - bravery

Bolt loves nothing more than racing and will do anything for his monster mates – except their homework!

MONSTER TRUCKS

FIZZ
SPEED - 99
BRAINS - 65
POWER - 30
SKILL - fast loop-the-loops

Step aside, here's Fizz! Small but speedy, Fizz is three-time winner of the Trucksville Drift & Style Cup.

MONSTER TRUCKS

NEWTON
SPEED - 95
BRAINS - 100
POWER - 42
SKILL - speaks 60 languages

Newton's brain is more powerful than a top-notch computer and he has a stylish crash helmet.

MONSTER TRUCKS

CHUNK
SPEED - 91
BRAINS - 22
POWER - 100
SKILL - pie-eating champion

Everyone loves Chunk! His brain is the size of a ping pong ball but he has a heart of pure gold.

ROXY
SPEED - 98
BRAINS - 89
POWER - 64
SKILL - skatepark champion

Streetwise Roxy is the queen of the skatepark and can successfully land a triple backflip.

MASHER
SPEED - 100
BRAINS - 67
POWER - 76
SKILL - cheeky pranks

Loud, fast and rather smelly, Masher is everyone's favourite bad boy. But not when he bends the rules…

The End